C000175899

Lin

SHARE

To

05211234

Bloomsbury Education
An imprint of Bloomsbury Publishing Plc

50 Bedford Square
London
WC1B 3DP
UK

1385 Broadway
New York
NY 10018
USA

www.bloomsbury.com

BLOOMSBURY and the Diana logo are trademarks of Bloomsbury Publishing Plc

First published in 2018

ISBN: PB: 978-1-4729-3490-1
ePub: 978-1-4729-3488-8
ePDF: 978-1-4729-3491-8

2 4 6 8 10 9 7 5 3 1

Typeset by Integra Software Services Pvt. Ltd.
Printed and bound in China by Leo Paper Products

To find out more about our authors and books visit www.bloomsbury.com.
Here you will find extracts, author interviews, details of forthcoming
events and the option to sign up for our newsletters.

recommended by

www.catchup.org

Catch Up is a charity which aims to address the problem of underachievement that
has its roots in literacy and numeracy difficulties

LIKE AND SHARE

JO COTTERILL

ILLUSTRATED BY
MARIA GARCIA BORREGO

BLOOMSBURY EDUCATION
AN IMPRINT OF BLOOMSBURY

LONDON OXFORD NEW YORK NEW DELHI SYDNEY

CONTENTS

Chapter One   7

Chapter Two   15

Chapter Three   21

Chapter Four   34

Chapter Five   41

Chapter Six   49

Chapter Seven   54

Chapter Eight   61

Chapter Nine   67

Chapter One

The moon shone over Hopewell High. It was 11pm, and everyone was supposed to be asleep. But in the dormitory called the Nest, Daisy was still awake. Daisy often found it hard to sleep.

Long after her friends Alice, Samira and Hani had fallen asleep, Daisy stared at the ceiling. Her brain was buzzing.

She decided to switch on her phone. She put her head under the duvet to hide the light, so as not to wake her friends. But who could she message? She gave a sigh. She missed talking to Storm, her ex-boyfriend. He'd been good fun, but in the end they were just too different. Daisy liked makeup, parties and shopping. Storm liked computer coding and rugby. After Storm, she'd fancied a boy at the gym. But he'd turned her down because he was gay. Daisy hated being without a boyfriend.

Then she had an idea and she smiled. Why not? She logged into a chatroom she hadn't visited for a while. It was for fans of an indie band, and there were usually lots of people up late wanting to talk.

Cutie has entered the chatroom

Tattoo405: CUUUUUTTTTTIIIIEEEE!!

Winterfairy: we haven't seen you in like YEARS!! What you been up to?

Cutie: hi guys! Oh you know not much. What's new today then?

Winterfairy: Tats's mum wants a new tattoo. I'll show you the options.

Images loading...

Cutie: I can't see anything, just three grey squares?

Winterfairy: oh this stupid computer. AAARGH!

Tattoo405: basically she's got it down to three — a unicorn, a rose twined round a book, or a ghost.

Cutie: wow they're pretty different.

Darkglasses: I said she could have a ghostly unicorn with a rose sticking out of its bum.

Cutie: hahaha!! I like it, tell your mum to have that Tats!

Tattoo405: yeah thanks DG, always got something SO helpful to say.

Darkglasses: *takes a bow*.

Winterfairy: oh look, our pet troll is back in the room ;)

Darkglasses: YOU HURT ME.

Cutie: if you're a troll, do you lurk under a bridge? Must be hard to see with dark glasses on.

Darkglasses: Ha! You're funny, cutie. Are you pretty too?

Cutie: who even are you? I'm sure I'd have remembered you from last time I was here...

Darkglasses: oh, I'm recent on here. Get bored easily, and I never sleep.

Cutie: me neither! ARE YOU REALLY ME?

Darkglasses: somehow I doubt it. If I were you, I'd be grabbing my own boobs.

Tattoo405: you are gross and insulting.

Darkglasses: it's what all boys would do if they were girls.

Cutie: you're funny ☺

Daisy smiled at the phone screen. She didn't know who Darkglasses was but he was just the kind of boy she liked to talk to – a bit of a rebel, not afraid to say what he was thinking. And then her smile grew wider as a new messaging window popped up.

Darkglasses has invited you to join a private conversation. Y/N?

Without hesitation, Daisy hit 'Y'.

Chapter Two

Sunlight streamed in through the windows of the Nest, but Daisy was still fast asleep. The other three were getting dressed. "She's going to miss breakfast," Samira said.

"Miss Redmond will be cross if she does," said Alice. The girls' house mistress did not like girls missing breakfast.

Hani picked up a pillow and threw it at Daisy's head. "Wake up, sleepy!"

"Huh? Wha...?" Daisy blinked and stared at them. Then she grunted and closed her eyes again. "It can't be morning."

"It is." Hani glanced out of the window. "You know that big yellow ball in the sky? It's called the sun. It comes up every morning. That's how you know it's morning and time to get up!"

Daisy threw the pillow back at Hani. "Go away," she croaked. "I'm sick."

"You're not." Alice pulled back Daisy's duvet. "Come on. Don't get in trouble."

"I am sick!" protested Daisy. Her eyes went all dreamy. "I'm **lovesick**..."

The other three girls groaned. "Not again!" said Samira.

Hani sat down on her bed with a thump. "Oh, go on, tell us. Since you're going to anyway!"

Daisy sat up and pushed her long dark hair out of her eyes. "I don't know his real name," she began. The others groaned again. "No, no, listen!" protested Daisy. "He's just the best thing ever. I got chatting to him last night online, and before I knew it, three hours had gone by. Three hours! I've never talked to anyone for that long before. He just totally gets me. He's into the same things. He really listens to me, you know?"

She sighed happily. "This is completely different from before. I really think he's the one."

Samira rolled her eyes. "If you spent as much time on your studies as you do on your boyfriends..."

"I'd be as dull as you," Daisy snapped. "Can't you just be happy for me?"

Samira stared at her, shocked. Without another word, she ran from the room.

"That was harsh, Daisy," said Alice.

Daisy looked ashamed for a moment. Then she frowned. "She's such a geek, that's all. She thinks education is the most important thing in the world."

"Well," said Hani slowly, "that's because where she comes from, it is. Iran isn't like England."

"I know that," Daisy said.

The school bell rang for breakfast. "You go," said Daisy, waving a hand. "I'll be down in five minutes."

Hani and Alice looked at each other and shrugged. Then they headed off down the corridor.

Daisy checked they'd gone and then picked up her phone. She'd finished chatting to Darkglasses at 2am! But as she unlocked the screen, she could see she had five new messages, all from him.

Daisy smiled, her heart filling with happiness. Her friends could sneer all they liked. But Daisy had a new boyfriend and he was PERFECT.

Chapter Three

Samira still wasn't talking to Daisy by the end of the day. "I wish you two would make up," Alice whispered to Daisy while they were doing their homework.

Daisy shook her head.

"We're just so different. She's a total egghead. A brainbox. A geek. I mean, she's great, but we just look at life in a completely different way. She's like my opposite." She leaned closer to Alice. "Here – do you want to see the photo that Darkglasses sent me?"

Alice took the phone under the table and peeked at it. On the screen was a photo of a lad in dark glasses. All you could really see of him was his eyebrows, his nose, and one corner of his mouth.

"Isn't he hot?" Daisy whispered.

Alice laughed. "Daisy, you can hardly see anything!"

"Girls!" Miss Redmond's voice was sharp. "No talking during prep!"

Daisy slipped the phone back into her pocket. She couldn't wait until bedtime so she could message Darkglasses again.

At bedtime, however, Hani said to her, "Daisy, you really should get some sleep. You've been yawning all day."

"Don't bother telling her," Alice said to Hani with a smile. "She won't listen to you. Look at her. She's already logging on!"

Samira said nothing, but got into bed and switched off her light.

Daisy didn't even hear the others trying to talk to her. She was already lying in bed, staring at her screen and smiling.

Darkglasses: hey cutie. Did you have a good day?

Cutie: not too bad. One of my friends isn't talking to me.

Darkglasses: You girls. Talking, not talking, friends, enemies...

Cutie: you mean frenemies.

Darkglasses: That word is NOT A REAL WORD!

Cutie: it is too! I guess Samira and I are frenemies sometimes. She's just so different.

Darkglasses: How so?

Cutie: she's really serious. She thinks studying is the most important thing ever. She gets annoyed if I don't do my homework.

Darkglasses: what is she, like, your mother?!

Cutie: I know!!

Darkglasses: I think you're quite serious underneath.

Cutie: me???

Darkglasses: yeah. You're all bubbly and social and funny but I think underneath there's another you.

Daisy stared at the screen, her heart thumping. No one had ever said that to her before. It was as if Darkglasses had seen straight through into the very middle of her. It made her feel... nervous.

Darkglasses: hey, you still there?

Cutie: yes.

Darkglasses: Did I say something wrong?

Cutie: no. Not at all. It's just... everyone only ever sees what's on the surface. No one has ever said there might be another me.

Darkglasses: well, am I right?

Cutie: you are.

Darkglasses: what's the 'other you' like?

Cutie: I'm nervous.

Darkglasses: why?

Cutie: this is like telling you all my secrets – I don't even know you! ;–)

Darkglasses: you want another photo?

Image loading...

Daisy opened her eyes very wide. He wasn't wearing his dark glasses this time. He was looking straight at the camera. He had very dark hair, dark eyes and the nicest lips she'd ever seen. Kissable lips. "Wow," she breathed.

Darkglasses: don't mention the spot on my chin

Cutie: what spot, where??

Darkglasses: DO NOT ENLARGE PHOTO it is as big as a volcano

Cutie: haha. I don't see it. You're gorgeous.

Darkglasses: wow, thanks. You really think so?

Cutie: don't you KNOW?

Darkglasses: I'm not really the popular sort. I don't exactly have girls falling at my feet.

Cutie: well I don't know why. I'd fall at your feet.

Darkglasses: careful! I might ask you to do that ;-)

Cutie: You wish!!!

Darkglasses: now you know what I look like. What about you? Send me a photo ☺

Cutie: what's your name first?

Darkglasses: seriously? It will be such a disappointment. Can't you think of me as the Mysterious Darkglasses?

Cutie: If you want a photo, tell me your name.

Darkglasses: oh, all right! It's Liam. See? Boring. Now send me a photo.

Cutie: it's dark. I'm in bed, all the lights are off.

Darkglasses: so? Switch them on!

Cutie: I can't, I'll wake up the other girls! Hang on, I'll find the flash. Here you go... it's terrible, I warn you.

Image loading...

Darkglasses: you look like a wild spirit

Cutie: I do? Is that a good thing?

Darkglasses: very good. You are one hot chick, cutie.

Cutie: Daisy. My name is Daisy.

Darkglasses: Hi Daisy ☺ Now that we've seen each other, tell me about the 'other you' that nobody knows... ;)

Chapter Four

In the days that followed, Daisy found she was thinking about Liam all the time. Every minute that she wasn't online with him, she missed him. He understood her like no one else ever had. He listened to her. He didn't talk about himself all the time.

He didn't tell her she was stupid if she didn't understand something.

Daisy found it hard to concentrate in lessons. She got told off more and more often. Miss Redmond, the house mistress, asked Daisy to come and see her. Daisy went into her office and sat down.

Miss Redmond smiled at her, but it was in a not-happy way. "I've been hearing things," she said. "Things from other teachers. You're not listening in lessons. You're not doing your homework. You look half-asleep too. Now, Daisy, this isn't good enough. You have a brain, but you're not using it. What's going on? Is there something the matter?"

Daisy looked at her. Miss Redmond was tall, with brown hair in a plait. She was a kind person, and she'd helped Daisy out in the past. But this time, Daisy couldn't tell her what was going on. She couldn't tell Miss Redmond that she was in love. Miss Redmond wouldn't understand. And if Miss Redmond knew how late she was staying up, she'd probably take away Daisy's phone. The very idea made Daisy feel sick. She couldn't lose touch with Liam!

"I'm fine," she said, with a shrug. "I'm just a bit bored, that's all."

"Bored?" repeated Miss Redmond, lifting her eyebrows.

"Yeah." Daisy pretended to yawn. "I just don't find the lessons very interesting at the moment."

"I see." Miss Redmond's lips pressed together in a straight line. Then she said, "May I remind you, Daisy, that your parents are paying for you to be here? They are paying for you to learn. They are not paying for you to be bored. I suggest you have a think about that, and change your attitude."

Daisy shrugged again. "Whatever."

Miss Redmond sounded very sharp now. "Consider this an official behaviour warning, Daisy. I will be keeping an eye on you."

"OK." Daisy got up and left. On the outside, she looked confident. On the inside, she felt like jelly. She couldn't believe she had just been so rude to her house mistress! And Miss Redmond was so nice, too! It made her feel awful.

Daisy climbed the stairs to the Nest. Her three friends were waiting for her. "What did she want?" asked Alice.

Daisy rolled her eyes. "Just wanted a moan." She grinned. "I told her I was well bored."

The other three looked shocked. "You did not!" said Alice. "Daisy, you'll be in so much trouble!"

"I don't care," said Daisy. "This place is so dull sometimes!"

Alice stared at her. "What's got into you?"

"It's that boy," said Samira suddenly. "She's obsessed."

"I am **not**," said Daisy, cross. "He's the best thing that's ever happened to me."

There was a pause.

"You used to say that about us," said Hani quietly. Then Daisy's three friends looked at each other and left the room.

Daisy sat down on her bed. She felt very upset. She hadn't meant to insult her friends. She wished she could tell them how Liam made

her feel; how he cared for her. How she loved every word he wrote. How she was trying to find a way to meet him – somehow, somewhere.

But she was afraid her friends would laugh. They had heard all about her boyfriends in the past. They wouldn't take her seriously – and yet, Daisy knew, **this** one was very serious. He saw through her confident side. He knew the real her, the one underneath. The one with worries and fears, just like everyone else.

Daisy wiped the tears from her face. So what if her friends had turned their backs on her? There was only one person she wanted to talk to now.

Daisy reached into her bag for her phone.

Chapter Five

Darkglasses: I'm so sorry, cutie. They don't sound like friends to me.

Cutie: I wish I could meet you, Liam. Where do you live?

Darkglasses: oh, miles away from you. Yorkshire.

Cutie: noooooooooooooooooo!! Come visit me ☺

Darkglasses: haha! Maybe I will one day ☺

Cutie: I'd love that. Sometimes I feel like you're the only one on my side.

Darkglasses: I am totally on your side. Which side? Do you have a best side?

Daisy laughed and took a selfie of the side of her face.

Image loading...

Darkglasses: That's a nice side! What's the other side like though, so I can compare?

Image loading...

Cutie: well?

Darkglasses: hmm. Let me study them more closely. Left... right... hmm. I think your right side is the best. But only by a tiny margin. Both sides are kissable.

Cutie: :-O

Darkglasses: what? Wouldn't you like me to kiss you?

Cutie: I SO would.

Darkglasses: send me a photo of where you'd like to be kissed.

Image loading...

Darkglasses: That's a very nice pair of lips. Have they seen a lot of action?

Cutie: Liam, you are so RUDE! You don't ask a girl things like that! ... A bit of action, yes ;-)

Darkglasses: Ha! I knew it! Daisy the naughty schoolgirl. Dirty Daisy.

Cutie: you're the one who started it...

Darkglasses: I want to know more. What does the rest of you look like?

Image loading...

Darkglasses: *wolf whistle* niiiiiiice. Rather too many clothes on though ;-P

Cutie: I'm not taking them off!!

Darkglasses: aw, go on. Just a bit. Show me a boob.

Cutie: no!!

Darkglasses: or a thigh.

Cutie: cheeky.

Darkglasses: a bra then. Show me your bra. That's nothing – you might as well be in a bikini.

Cutie: oh, all right. Hang on...

Darkglasses: you're taking ages! I'm dying here!

Cutie: I've taken 14 and none of them are nice!

Darkglasses: send me all 14 and I'll see if I agree with you.

Cutie: I'll send you ONE.

Image loading...

Darkglasses: PHWOOOOOOOAAAARRRR!

Cutie: LOL. Is that all right?

Darkglasses: you look amazing. Hiding those under your school uniform!! What I wouldn't give to get my hands on them...

Cutie: you're in Yorkshire, remember. No chance ☹

Darkglasses: ☹

Cutie: gotta go. Can hear someone coming

Darkglasses: thanks for the photo. I'll be looking at it last thing tonight ☺

Cutie: xxx

Chapter Six

Two days later, Daisy was in the ICT Room at lunchtime. She was supposed to be catching up on her homework. Instead she was editing a photo of herself on her phone. She liked sending Liam photos.

Nothing naked – but it wasn't hurting anyone to show him her underwear, was it? And he loved it. He told her she was beautiful; he couldn't wait to meet her one day.

A burst of giggles from further down the room made her look up. Three girls from the year below were gathered around a computer. They were sneaking glances at Daisy and looking back at the computer screen – and then giggling.

"What?" asked Daisy, annoyed.

But the girls were giggling so hard they couldn't even speak. Then one of them gasped out, "Nice bra," and they were all helpless with laughter again.

Daisy sat very still. She felt as though someone had tipped a bucket of iced water over her head. It couldn't be...

Somehow, she got up. Somehow she made her way over to the girls' computer. Still giggling, they backed off, and then disappeared – probably to spread the gossip all over the school.

Daisy looked at the screen.

The site was called 'What Do You Think Of My Girlfriend?' and there, in the middle of the page, was the photo she had sent to Liam two nights earlier. The one of her with her shirt fully unbuttoned. She was pouting at the screen, pushing her lips together like a kiss – and her bra was on full display.

Daisy clutched at the chair, feeling dizzy. What was all this about?

Underneath the photo was a caption: 'Dirty Daisy, aged 14. Whaddya think, lads?'

And under that were the comments... oh, so many comments.

Daisy began to read, but the language used made her choke. Everything in the photo was commented on, from the design of her bra to the size of her breasts, to the shape of her face.

And then there were the comments from boys saying what they'd like to do to her...

The bile rose in her throat, and Daisy made it to the bin just in time to throw up.

There was only one person who could have posted that photo online.

The one person she had trusted more than any other.

Chapter Seven

Daisy ran up to the Nest, ignoring the bell for afternoon lessons. She felt sick and cold and terrified. How could he do this to her? That was a private photo, not to be shared with the world!

To think that all those other boys – and men – had seen her in her underwear... and that some of them even wanted to...

Liam had put her name and age, for goodness' sake! Was she even safe? Could anyone using the site find out who she was and where she went to school? Why would Liam do such a horrible, horrible thing? She sent him a message.

Cutie: How could you?? HOW COULD YOU????? I TRUSTED YOU!

Daisy lay in bed, sobbing. It felt like hours before anyone came looking for her – and then it was Miss Redmond.

The teacher came into the room and shut the door behind her. "Daisy," she said kindly. "Daisy, we need to talk."

"I can't," Daisy mumbled.

"This is very serious," Miss Redmond went on. "Can you tell me what happened?"

"I'm so embarrassed," Daisy said into her pillow.

"I know," Miss Redmond said. "I would be too. But you can't hide in bed for the rest of your life. Come out and tell me. You'll feel better."

Daisy sat up. Her face was puffy and red from all the crying, and her throat was sore.

"I got talking to a boy online," she said. "I thought he liked me. He – I stayed up late chatting to him. He wanted photos of me, so I sent them."

"Oh, Daisy," said Miss Redmond, shaking her head.

Daisy felt a spark of anger. "Everyone does it!" she cried. "If you've got a boyfriend, you

send him photos – they want it. And they send you photos back. It's called a **relationship**."

"It's called breaking the law," corrected Miss Redmond.

Daisy stared at her. "What?"

"It's against the law to take a photo of a child under 18 that has a sexual style," Miss Redmond said. "Such as a photo of you in your bra, pouting at the camera."

"But I took it **myself**!" Daisy protested.

"It's still against the law," Miss Redmond told her. "It's also against the law to send it to someone else."

"What about him uploading my photo to a website?" Daisy just felt angry now. "That's **way** worse."

"If you hadn't sent him the photo in the first place, he couldn't have done it," Miss Redmond pointed out. "But yes, it was against the law for him to do that too."

There was a silence.

"Am I... am I going to prison?" asked Daisy in a small voice. Tears started to run down her face again.

Miss Redmond smiled. "No, Daisy, I don't suppose so. But we have a responsibility to take this very seriously. We have to report it to the police. And we'll need to call your parents."

"Oh please, no!" Daisy covered her face with her hands. "Can't we just pretend it never happened? I won't do it again, I promise."

"It's too late," said Miss Redmond. "I'm very sorry, Daisy. We'll need to write to the site that's hosting your photo too and ask them to take it down." She got up. "I'm going to send one of your friends up to keep you company for this afternoon. I have to talk to the Head, and we'll need to make some phone calls to the right people. We'll try to get that photo taken down as quickly as possible. You don't have to come to lessons, but I will expect to see you at supper later."

"All right," said Daisy, sniffing.

"Which friend would you like me to send up?" Miss Redmond asked.

Daisy opened her mouth to say, "Alice", but the word didn't come out. Instead, she knew exactly who would understand. "Samira," she said. "Samira, please."

Chapter Eight

"Why me?" Samira asked when she came into the Nest. "Why not Alice?"

Daisy sat on her bed, hugging her knees. "Do you know what's happened?" she asked.

Samira nodded. "It's all over the school. Sorry."

Daisy took a deep breath. "I wanted to talk to you. Because... because you understand what it's like when people find out your secret."

"Oh." Samira sat down on the end of her own bed. "Oh, I see."

"You remember..." Daisy swallowed, "when we found out about your self-harm?"

Samira said quietly, "This isn't the same."

"No," agreed Daisy. "But I still feel... ashamed. Like you did."

Samira looked straight at her friend. "You know we can still be friends though, right?"

Daisy chewed the end of her hair. "I've been so stupid. I just want to be liked. I hate it when no one notices me. I want boys to fancy me. Why is that wrong?"

"It's not wrong," said Samira carefully, "but if it's all you think about, then maybe you've got a problem."

Daisy nodded. "I trusted someone I shouldn't. I thought... I thought he loved me, Sammy. I really did."

Samira came over and put an arm around Daisy's shoulders. "You don't value yourself enough," she told her. "You work so hard on the way you look. But that's not what people are really about. Who are you underneath?"

Daisy felt surprised. Only Liam had asked her that question. She'd thought no one else would be interested. "I don't know," she said slowly. "What if there **isn't** anything underneath? What if a face, and a body – and a bra – is all that I am?"

Samira smiled. "You think Hani, Alice and I are friends with your **bra**?"

Daisy couldn't help laughing at that. "I just want a boyfriend," she confessed. "I feel lonely without one. I need someone to tell me I'm gorgeous all the time. Otherwise I feel invisible."

Samira looked at her for a long moment. Then she said, "I think maybe you need to go talk to the counsellor. That sounds all kinds of wrong to me."

At the end of lessons, Alice and Hani came to join them. There was lots of hugging and crying and Daisy felt a lot better. Her friends weren't walking out on her because of what she'd done.

Going down to supper was really awkward though. **Everyone** knew, that much was clear. Gossip spread fast in a school. Daisy kept her eyes on the floor but she could still hear the whispers around her. And she definitely heard the girl that said, "That's disgusting," in a loud voice.

Samira reached for Daisy's hand and squeezed it. "It will get better," she whispered to her friend. "Be strong, Daisy."

Daisy didn't think she had ever felt less strong.

Chapter Nine

Darkglasses: what did I do?? What are you talking about?

Cutie: You posted that photo of me online! You are VILE.

Darkglasses: It was cute! I wanted everyone to see what a hot girlfriend I have!

Cutie: You DIDN'T ASK MY PERMISSION.

Darkglasses: Babe – Daisy – I didn't think you'd mind. You sent it to me, after all. What's the difference?

Cutie: The difference??! You can't even SEE what you've done to me? Everyone at school knows – I am humiliated. Even my PARENTS know.

Darkglasses: Aw, poor cutie! Don't worry. They'll have forgotten about it by tomorrow ;–)

Cutie: They won't. This will stay around forever. Did you know, once you upload a photo, you lose control of it? It's not yours any more. Anyone can copy it, share it... did you know that photo of me is now on SIX other websites?

Darkglasses: Whoa, really? LOL, have you been searching the web?

Cutie: I didn't need to. The police told me.

Darkglasses: The police?

Cutie: See, you're scared now, aren't you? You should be. You've broken the law.

Darkglasses: You told them about me? You bitch!

Cutie: Call me whatever names you like. They're coming for you, Liam. They can track everything.

Darkglasses: I never liked you. It was all pretend. All that stuff you told me – I was laughing at you while I read it. You fell for me SO easily.

Cutie: I'd rather be foolish than evil.

Darkglasses: You're pathetic, Daisy. Even your friends know it.

Cutie: Actually, my friends are amazing. They're the best thing ever. Do you have friends, Liam? Because I think you're going to need them. I feel sorry for you, getting off on telling lies. How many other girls have you done this to? How many lies have you told?

Darkglasses: This isn't about me. This is about you. It was ALL about you. You never shut up talking about yourself.

Cutie: Well, I'm shutting up now. I've said everything I wanted to say. The police will be interested in what you said too.

Darkglasses: You're going to show them this??

Cutie: Don't need to. I gave them access to my account. They can see everything. They can see YOU, Liam. Yeah, the world may be seeing me in my bra, but you know what? You're the one who'll be exposed.

Darkglasses: Your boobs are too small anyway.

Cutie: Goodbye, Liam.

Daisy logged out of the conversation and deleted her account. Her heart was racing and her hands were slippery with sweat, but she felt proud. Liam was a toad, a parasite; she deserved better. She still didn't want to face the world. That photo would be out there forever now – anyone could find it, even in ten, twenty, thirty years' time. "Thank goodness I wasn't naked," she thought to herself. She sat up on her bed and brushed her hair with shaking hands.

"Hey Daisy," called Alice, "you coming to the Common Room?"

"Oh," said Daisy, "I'm not sure..." The Common Room would be full of girls. Girls who would look at her and whisper about her, and judge her.

"It's Friday night," said Hani. "Film night!"

"Come on," said Samira. She held out a hand and smiled. "We'll be right there with you."

Daisy took a deep breath. She couldn't hide forever. Feeling sick with nerves, she got up and took Samira's hand. It was warm and strong, and Daisy instantly felt braver.

Together, the four friends walked out of the Nest – stronger together, forever.

Bonus Bits!

WHAT NEXT?

Have a think about these questions after
reading this story:

- What do you think Daisy should have
  done when she was asked to send a photo
  to Darkglasses?

- Do you think Samira was right to
  suggest Daisy sees a counsellor when she
  explained how she saw herself?

- Were Daisy's friends right to stand by her
  after the event?

- How do you think Samira felt towards
  Daisy throughout the story?

CONSENT AND THE LAW

Consent is agreeing to something of your own free will, not because someone is putting pressure on you. In a relationship, it can be hard to say no because you want the other person to like you. But legally you have the right to refuse a request, whether it's for a photo of yourself or sexual contact you're not ready for. You should also respect that your partner might say no sometimes too.

If you are under 18, it is against the law for anyone to take or have a sexual photo of you – **even if it's a selfie** (like Daisy in the story). So, if you (like Darkglasses) put pressure on someone to take a photo or you share a sexual photo with someone, you're breaking the law.

WHERE TO GET HELP

Daisy likes to be noticed but she gets into trouble when she finds that she has broken the law. Luckily her friends are there for her and adults are able to help her. If you have concerns and worries about consent or anything else, there are people outside of your immediate family and friends who can help.

Childline

Childline is a free, 24-hour counselling service for everyone under 18. Childline says, "You can talk to us about anything. No problem is too big or too small. We're on the phone and online.

However you choose to contact us, you're in control. It's free, confidential and you don't have to give your name if you don't want to."

www.childline.org.uk / telephone: 0800 1111

Mind

Mind is a charity for people with mental health problems. It can provide help and information if you or someone you know feels bad about themselves like Daisy does. It is for adults and children.

www.mind.org.uk / telephone: 0300 123 3393 / text: 86463